To Zoey and Iker and their sidekicks, Gwyneth and Lucia —K. N.

For Baron Aranda and family, who make a super team!—K. Y.

STERLING CHILDREN'S BOOKS
New York

An Imprint of Sterling Publishing Co., Inc.
1166 Avenue of the Americas
New York, NY 10036

STERLING CHILDREN'S BOOKS and the distinctive Sterling Children's Books logo are
registered trademarks of Sterling Publishing Co., Inc.

Text © 2018 Kim Norman
Cover and interior illustrations © 2018 Keika Yamaguchi

ISBN 978-1-4549-2358-9

Distributed in Canada by Sterling Publishing Co., Inc.
C/o Canadian Manda Group, 664 Annette Street
Toronto, Ontario M6S 2C8, Canada
Distributed in the United Kingdom by GMC Distribution Services
Castle Place, 166 High Street, Lewes, East Sussex BN7 1XU, England
Distributed in Australia by NewSouth Books
45 Beach Street, Coogee, NSW 2034, Australia

For information about custom editions, special sales, and premium and corporate purchases,
please contact Sterling Special Sales at 800-805-5489 or specialsales@sterlingpublishing.com.

Manufactured in China

Lot #:
2 4 6 8 10 9 7 5 3 1
10/18

sterlingpublishing.com

Cover and interior design by Irene Vandervoort

The illustrations were drawn with pencil and painted digitally.

THUNDER PUG

by
KIM NORMAN

illustrated by
KEIKA YAMAGUCHI

STERLING CHILDREN'S BOOKS
New York

Percy was a pug, and Petunia was a pig. Even so, they loved doing many of the same things:

Carving trails through lanky weeds,

puffing dandelion seeds,

playing twilight hide-and-seek,

lapping puddles,
cheek to cheek.

Of course, Percy didn't do everything with Petunia.

Sometimes Percy did pug things while Petunia did pig things.

And Percy was content
to wave good-bye

as Petunia rode off to the
Arlington County Fair.

HOORAY PETUNIA!

When she returned wearing a blue ribbon,

Percy was proud of her.

So was everyone else.

He offered a high-five but missed.

He offered flowers and was nearly trampled.

Even the kiss he blew floated away, lost on the wind.

Petunia wore her ribbon everywhere.

Seriously—everywhere.

It seemed to Percy that she had no time
for puddles, or dandelions, or . . . him.

One day, as Percy sat alone in a puddle, he spotted something peculiar.

Percy pored over the faded pages.

THUNDER MAN

Thunder Man was strong and brave.

He saved plunging planes.

WHOOSH!

He rescued sinking sailors.

And he had something just as special as a first-prize ribbon: He had a cape.

Percy had an idea.

Sometimes being Thunder Pug was exciting.

Sometimes it was messy.

Sometimes it even tickled.

And yet, somehow,
it was never quite . . . satisfying.

What was he doing wrong? Percy flipped through his book.
On page six, where Thunder Man saves a school bus, Percy
noticed something:

Thunder Man had something better than a cape.
He had a sidekick!

Percy looked up.
There, in all her blue-ribbon glory, was . . .

PINK LIGHTNING!

And just in time.

Thunder Pug and Pink Lightning
to the rescue!

HELP!

Percy offered his back, and Petunia climbed aboard.

She stretched and
stretched and stretched . . .

. . . and plopped
into some
prickly plants.
Ouch!

As pig and pug struggled and tugged . . .

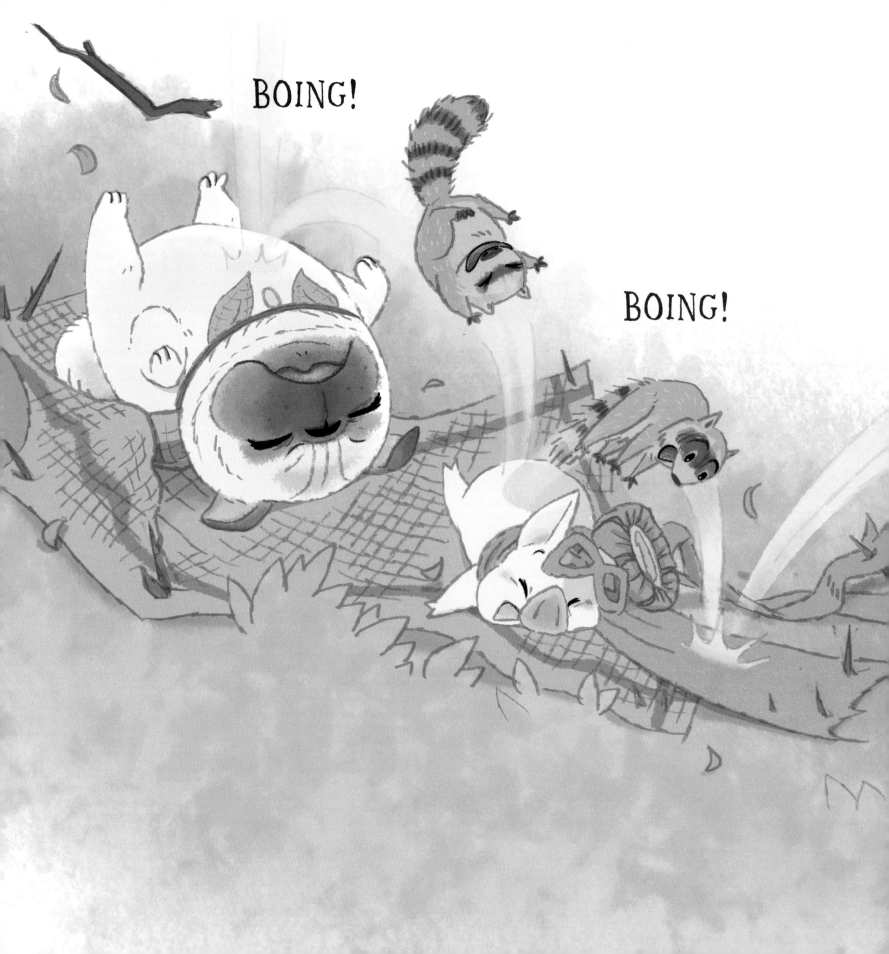

WHEEEE!!!!

While Percy and Petunia untangled themselves (with a little help), they learned something new:

The heroic life can be satisfying indeed . . . when you're side by sidekick.

Like when you're helping:

Beetles climbing
swaying flowers,

spiderwebs in
heavy showers,

hedgehogs lost in
purple clover,

turtles who need
turning over.

Percy is still a pug, and Petunia is still a pig,
so sometimes he does pug things
while she does pig things.

But when they are together,
they're perfectly . . .

... THUNDERFUL.